Disney Girls

One Pet Too Many

Gabrielle Charbonnet

N E W   Y O R K

Printed in the United States of America.

First Edition

1 3 5 7 9 10 8 6 4 2

The text of this book is set in 15-point Adobe Garamond.

Library of Congress Catalog Card Number: 98-84793

ISBN: 0-7868-4166-4

For more Disney Press fun, visit www.DisneyBooks.com

Contents

Chapter One

My Animal Spirit

How to make acorn earrings:

1) Find two acorns. (Green ones work best.)
2) Remove their little caps.
3) First rub one end, then the other, on the sidewalk. Wear down both sides until you're left with a thin ring shape.
4) Pop the acorn meat out of the ring and slit the ring with your fingernail.
5) Carefully spread the slit and clip it to your earlobe. *Voila!*

Making acorn earrings is just one of the cool things my friends and I do when we're having a Pocahontas day. (My name is Paula Pinto, a.k.a. Pocahontas.) Today my five best friends and I had been living in Pocahontas's magical world. We had been practicing running silently through the trees in Willow Green, watching the clouds, making acorn earrings, and having a snack of dried fruit and pecans harvested from my own backyard. Now there was something else I wanted to try.

"Come on, guys," I called. I spread out my Southwestern blanket beneath an oak tree and sat cross-legged on it. Since we live in Orlando, Florida, the ground wasn't that cold, even though it was January. But the blanket is still nice.

The five other Disney Girls ran toward me from all over Willow Green. (I'll explain about being Disney Girls and about Pocahontas in a minute.) Willow Green is a small park that's right in the middle of Willow Hill, the suburb of Orlando where all of us live. I mean, almost all of us. Jasmine Prentiss lives in Wildwood Estates. But she's at our houses so much it feels like she lives here, too.

Ariel Ramos (she's my *best* best friend) ran up first and flopped down on a corner of the blanket. Her long red hair had a few leaves in it, and she had lost one of her acorn earrings. Next came Isabelle Beaumont, then Yukiko Hayashi, Ella O'Connor, and Jasmine. I rubbed my hands together happily. We were all here.

"What now, Pocahontas?" asked Ariel.

"I want us to try to get in touch with our animal spirits," I said. "Let's sit in a circle."

I smiled when I noticed that the three pairs of *best* best friends automatically sat next to each other: me and Ariel, Yukiko and Ella, and Isabelle and Jasmine.

"What's an animal spirit?" asked Yukiko.

"In my tribe," I explained, "people often identify with different animals. Like, someone might be as brave as a cougar, as silent as a fox, or as strong as a bear. I thought it would be kind of kickin' for us to close our eyes and concentrate. Then the first animal you see when you open your eyes will be your animal spirit. At least for today."

It's true that I'm Pocahontas in my "real," Disney Girl life. But in my everyday life, I am actually Native American (mostly of the Seminole tribe). Which explains my dark brown hair and brown eyes.

"Cool," said Jasmine.

"Let's do it," Ella agreed.

3

"You know, we're not exactly in the wild," Ariel pointed out. "I mean, there aren't that many cougars, foxes, and bears hanging out in Willow Green. I don't want to open my eyes and see, like, a roly-poly bug."

Isabelle pretended to roll up into a terrified ball. "Oh, no!" she squeaked in a high, buggy voice. "Humans!"

When we finally stopped giggling, we got down to business. Sitting in a circle, we linked pinkies and closed our eyes. (Linking pinkies connects us. It draws more magic to us, and reminds us that not only are we connected to each other, but we're part of everything in the whole world.)

I breathed in the soft air and focused my mind. When I thought we'd had enough time to get in touch with our animal spirits, I said quietly, "Jasmine? You go first."

Jasmine's green eyes instantly fixed on something straight ahead. I looked also and saw a girl riding a beautiful dark horse on one of the bridle paths that run around the edge of Willow Green.

"Awesome," said Jasmine with a smile. "I'm a horse."

"What does *that* mean?" asked Ella.

"Think about a horse's traits," I suggested.

4

"Um, okay, it means . . . I'm fast, powerful, and graceful," said Jasmine. "All *right*."

I grinned at her. "Let's close our eyes again and focus."

Next was Isabelle's turn. When we opened our eyes, Isabelle immediately saw an orange, white, and black cat slinking through the grass.

"Great," Isabelle giggled. "I'm sneaky, quiet, and determined. I'm also calico."

"Yep, that's you, all right," Yukiko said. "I just wish you'd quit eating lizards. So gross."

We couldn't stop laughing. Isabelle is about the most ungross person I could think of. She's African American, and really pretty and together.

I was really hyped by what was happening. Curiosity was burning through me. What animal would I see for myself? Again we closed our eyes for a few minutes. "Ari—" I began, but was interrupted by Ariel sneezing.

"Ah—ah—choo!" Her eyes flew open. "Oh, no!" she wailed.

Five heads swiveled to see the problem. One by one, we tried to stifle our laughter, but it was no use. Nearby, a man was trying to walk his Irish setter puppy, but he was having a hard time. The puppy was leaping and pulling on its leash. Yipping and bouncing, its long, shiny red coat gleamed in the thin winter sunlight. The puppy ignored its owner and strained to be free.

Ariel held her head with her hands.

"I don't think there's any question about this one," I said, snickering. "That puppy is Ariel—no doubt about it."

"It's like looking into a mirror, isn't it?" asked Ella.

"Let's just move on," Ariel grumbled.

Yukiko's turn was next. When we opened our eyes, she was scanning the sky. Above us was a small hawk, wheeling through the clear blue heavens.

"Whoa," whispered Yukiko as we all watched the beautiful, fierce bird. "Could I really be so wild and free?" Her dark, almond-shaped eyes shone.

I shivered as a tingle of magic went up my spine.

"My turn," said Ella eagerly, and closed her eyes. As I concentrated, feeling the magic swirling around me like leaves in a winter wind, I heard her whisper, "Please let it be a good animal."

"Okay," she said, and my eyes snapped open. At first Ella looked confused, then she frowned.

"Figures," she said with a sigh. I looked to where she

6

was pointing. A small gray squirrel sat on a nearby branch. It was nibbling an acorn held between its paws. Its bright black eyes watched us with curiosity.

Yukiko chuckled. "Now, is this the 'before' squirrel, or the 'after' squirrel?" We laughed, because Ella is Cinderella (yes, *that* Cinderella), and just last month she had decided to give herself a makeover. Now she looked like the "after" Cinderella, with new clothes, a new hair-cut, and everything.

Frowning thoughtfully, Ariel asked, "Ella, do you think this will help you get in touch with your inner rodent?" She sneezed again.

Isabelle fell over laughing. I pounded the blanket, laughing so hard I could barely breathe.

"Oh, ha-ha," said Ella sourly. "You guys are soooo funny. Let's see how well *you* do, Pocahontas. I bet you look up to see a . . . a . . . *cockroach* or something."

I was gasping for air. The others were laughing so loudly that joggers were turning to look at us. A cock-roach!

"Of course, here in Florida," I choked out, "the roaches are almost bigger than the squirrels. So it wouldn't be too bad."

Like five minutes later we were ready for me to actually take my turn. I felt excited and expectant, as if something important and magical was about to happen. I hoped I *wouldn't* see a cockroach! Or a mosquito. Or a duck! There were ducks in the park lagoon, and they wandered all over the place. I sure didn't feel like a duck.

"Ready?" asked Jasmine.

"Ready," I said, and opened my eyes. At first I didn't see anything. Just a bush. I was about to look around, but the bush moved. A scaly pinkish nose poked out from underneath the leaves. I peered closer. What was I seeing?

I sat back in surprise. "I'm an armadillo!"

Chapter Two

Our Magical Secret

"Really? An armadillo?" Isabelle said, scrambling to her feet. Instantly we had surrounded the little animal.

"Keep back—don't spook it," I warned. I looked closer. It was an armadillo, all right. They're pretty common here in Florida, but I had never seen one right in my own neighborhood.

"What's it doing here?" Ariel whispered.

I shook my head. "I don't know. Maybe it's lost. It shouldn't even be awake right now—they're usually nocturnal."

"That means they sleep during the day and are awake at night, right?" asked Ella softly.

"Uh-huh," I answered. Usually armadillos are pretty shy, but this one didn't even seem to know we were there. I knew they didn't see or hear well, especially in daylight, but surely it could smell us. What was wrong? Then I gasped and pointed. One of its paws was bloody! The armadillo held it close to its body. Silently I counted only three toes.

"It's missing a toe!" I said. "It got injured somehow."

"What should we do?" asked Yukiko.

I pinched my lip and thought about it. One thing you should know about me is that I am completely crazy about animals—all animals. My whole family is. In fact, my mom was studying right now to take her final qualifying test to become a veterinarian. I want to be one, too, when I grow up.

"Paula?" pressed Ariel.

"I'm going to take it home to have my mom look at it," I quickly decided. I whipped off my jeans jacket. "Wow, it's about the size of a big house cat. But armadillos don't bite—they don't even have front teeth," I explained. "But they can jump really high when they're startled, and they have big sharp claws for digging. So . . . I'll sneak up behind it and throw my jacket over it."

I told my friends to get ready with my heavy blanket, in case I missed the armadillo. They could throw the blanket over it and I could try again.

But they didn't need to. The poor little animal stood trembling and confused as I slipped up behind it and scooped it into my jeans jacket. Then I cradled it firmly in my arms, trying to avoid its hurt paw.

The six of us started for my house. As we walked down Church Street, I thought again about how lucky I was to have found all my best friends. This seems like a good time to tell you how we all met. The first one I became friends with was Ariel. We had lived around the corner from each other all our lives, but had never met.

Then, when I was six, I was riding my new bike. Just around the corner, in front of a big white house, a red-headed girl had set up a small ramp for her own bicycle. I could see that she had wiped out a bunch of times—her knees were skinned. But she hadn't given up. She looked pretty determined.

The ramp looked like fun. So, without saying anything,

11

I rode my own bike into position. Then I hunched over the handlebars, raced up the ramp, and flew off the end. I landed hard about five feet away and spun a little, but didn't drop my bike.

The redheaded girl looked amazed—and happy. She ran over to me. "You're my real sister!" she cried. I just grinned. I felt that way, too.

From then on, Ariel and I were best friends. She was so much more fun than the girls I had met in first grade! Just like me, she liked to run hard, climb high, and get dirty. We rode our bikes, learned to skate together, and had water balloon fights.

At the same time, Ariel was in kindergarten with Yukiko and Ella. They were already best friends, too, and sometimes Ariel played with them. Soon the four of us were hanging out together. Yukiko and Ella are much quieter and less athletic than Ariel or I. Back then they liked to have little tea parties and play with their dolls or stuffed animals. Still, there was something about them that I really liked. They were fun and fun to hang out with and totally cool. We just fit well together, even though I knew we were so different.

One rainy day, we found out what all four of us had

in common. I had rented the movie *Pocahontas*, and we settled down in my family room to watch it. Now I'll tell you a secret: The first time I saw *Pocahontas* at the movie theater, it was almost scary. It was like someone had followed me around, filming me, and then put it up on the screen. In one instant I just *knew* I *was* Pocahontas. Not just like, not similar, not sort of. I mean, I *was*. I *am*.

But I kept those feelings inside. They felt private, and I don't usually go around blabbing all my feelings anyway. I hadn't even told Ariel about it, even though I always told her everything.

So, that day at my house, we were all watching *Pocahontas*. I was sitting there with my eyes locked on the screen. Magical shivers were making all the little hairs on my arms stand up. I felt like if I touched something, tiny blue sparks would fly.

Suddenly, Yukiko whispered, "It's you. That's you up on the TV. You're Pocahontas."

It was like the sky had broken open and split my world with lightning. I stared at Yukiko, and then Ella nodded, her hand to her cheek. "I see it, too," she said.

That was the day that changed our lives. I paused the

movie and poured out all my feelings about Pocahontas, and how I really am her. I was shocked when Yukiko admitted that she felt the same way about Snow White! Even her name means *snow* in Japanese! Then Ariel pulled out her *Little Mermaid* backpack. When I saw it right next to her, I put it all together: how she loves to swim, has a bunch of sisters, has long red hair . . . you get the idea. So I was Pocahontas, Ariel was Ariel, the Little Mermaid; and Yukiko was Snow White. We all turned to look at Ella.

"I'm Cinderella," she announced. "I've always been Cinderella. Cinder*ella*, get it?"

We got it, but good. We sat around with silly grins on our faces, enjoying the magic that had just entered our lives.

Last year, Yukiko met Jasmine at ballet class and got a special, funny feeling about her. It wasn't long before we realized that beneath Jasmine's blond hair and green eyes was Princess Jasmine from *Aladdin*.

The last Disney Girl was Isabelle Beaumont. We met her just this year, when she transferred to our school, Orlando Elementary. Isabelle and Jasmine became best friends—and then we realized that Isabelle was Belle, from *Beauty and the Beast*. (Her next-door neighbor, Kenny McIlhenny, is the Beast.)

Cool, huh? More like awesome. The six of us are magic, we're princesses, and we're best friends. We're the Disney Girls, and we always will be.

Chapter Three

Dr. Jennifer

"Well?" I asked anxiously.

Mom's forehead crinkled into little lines as she carefully examined the armadillo. We were in my family's dining room. This room doesn't usually get much use, since we always eat in the kitchen. The dining room table is always covered with Mom's textbooks, Dad's engineering papers, and right now, an armadillo.

"She's badly dehydrated and thin," said Mom. "Her side is bruised, and you're right, she *is* missing a front toe. I think maybe she got hit by a car several days ago, and has been wandering around since then."

I drew in a sharp breath. I told you I loved animals, but sometimes the word *love* doesn't even cover it. Animals and I are connected, the same way the Disney Girls and I are. When an animal feels pain, it hurts me, too. Now the thought of this poor, frightened, and hungry armadillo made me feel terrible.

"Poor thing!" I said, hearing a catch in my voice. "What can we do?"

Just then, one of our dogs, Duchess, came nosing up to the table. Duchess is a greyhound and used to be a racing dog. We adopted her when she retired.

"Careful, Duchess," I warned softly. The armadillo didn't move.

"Hmm, look at that," said Mom. "The armadillo is either too dazed to be afraid, or has been around dogs before."

"Maybe it's a pet who got lost," suggested Ariel. "Ah-choo!"

Ella handed her a tissue. "You've been sneezing all afternoon."

Duchess sniffed the armadillo, then loped away. All of our pets are pretty laid-back. We have two other dogs besides Duchess—another retired greyhound named

17

Jazzhot and a three-legged beagle named Bobby. We also have three cats: Stopit, Getdown, and Nomore. My dad named them. Plus we have four tiny finches in a birdcage in our dining room, and my brother, Damon, keeps fish in an aquarium in his room. (Damon is fourteen. He's really cool.)

Last, and certainly not least, is my special pet: my raccoon, Meeko. (Guess where I got the name!) Dad found him when he was just a tiny baby. His mom had gotten killed by a car. (I almost freaked when I heard that.) I bottle-fed him until he could eat real food, and he's been with us ever since.

Most of the time, all our pets get along great. But every once in a while one of them has a hissy fit and they all freak out. Then they calm down again. My life would feel really empty without my pets.

"Ah-choo!" sneezed Ariel.

"Are you coming down with something?" I asked. She shrugged.

"Okay," said my mom. "I've cleaned her wound and put antibiotic cream on it. I'm also going to give her a shot of antibiotics. Then I guess we should fix her up a nice box on the screened porch."

"Great!" I said. That's one of the super things about my mom. Some parents wouldn't even allow an armadillo in the house, but Mom is into animals just as much as I am. I can't wait till she takes her final exams and is finally a full-fledged vet.

Half an hour later, the Disney Girls checked out the armadillo one last time. I had found a big cardboard box and lined it with an old blanket. We gave her a dish of water and cut up some fruit and vegetables. Armadillos also eat a lot of insects, but we didn't happen to have any around just now.

"Okay, guys," I said softly. "We better split and let her get settled. She might not eat if we're around. Let's go hang in my room for a while."

My room is pretty small, just like Isabelle's room. In fact, our houses are a lot alike. The rooms are laid out in the same way, and Isabelle's bedroom and mine are in exactly the same place. But inside, our houses are way different. Isabelle's parents are into white walls and cool African art. Everything is always in its place at her house. It seems a little unrelaxed, if you know what I mean.

Our house, on the other hand, is *really* relaxed. To tell you the truth, neither of my parents is into housekeeping. I mean, we don't live in a total pigsty. But we all have a lot of stuff, and it's hard to keep it put away just so. Plus, with three dogs, three cats, a raccoon, birds, fish, and now an armadillo, trying to keep the place neat would be a losing battle.

In my room the walls are painted a soft pinkish-tan color. I picked it out myself. I wanted it to look like the sky at dawn, right when the sun is coming up. I have a Southwestern blanket on my bed (the one I took to the park), and posters of animals and Native American things on the walls. My dad, Will, besides being an engineer, is almost completely Seminole Indian. (He says he had an English great-great-grandfather.) My mom, Jennifer, is one-quarter white, one-quarter Seminole, and half Cawtawba Indian. (The Cawtawbas live mostly in South Carolina. Florida has a lot of Seminoles.) Once I tried to figure out exactly what I was, but it gave me a headache. I'm just myself.

Ariel threw herself down on my bed and sneezed again.

"Ugh," she groaned, wiping her nose. "Maybe I *am* coming down with something. I don't really feel bad, but I can't stop sneezing."

We all made sympathetic faces at her.

"So!" said Ella, swinging her feet against my bed. "Do you think you're going to keep the armadillo?"

"Sure," I said, shrugging. "We almost always keep animals that are injured. Like Bobby." Bobby had also been hit by a car, which is why he has only three legs. It's amazing how fast he can run. And he can still jump up onto our beds and couches and stuff, even though he's not supposed to.

"You have to name her," said Yukiko.

"Yeah," Ariel agreed. "Like Armie, or Dilly."

I rolled my eyes. "Could you get a *little* more lame, please?"

"Name her Paula, since she's your animal spirit," said Jasmine, giggling.

I ignored her. "Maybe Pearl," I mused, "since she's like a little pink jewel."

"Hmm," said Isabelle. "'Jewel' might be stretching it a little. She's kind of . . . scaly."

"How about Rose? Or Daisy?" I suggested. I've always liked flower names. As soon as I said it, I knew Daisy was the right one. "That's it! I'll name her Daisy." I sat back, happy with that choice.

"Sounds good to me. I better go," Ariel said foggily. "I

don't want to get germs all over you guys." She sneezed again, right next to Isabelle. Isabelle stared at her arm and frowned.

"Sorry," said Ariel. "See you guys tomorrow at school, 'kay?"

"'Kay," I agreed, walking her to the door. "I hope you feel better. Thanks for helping with Daisy."

"No prob," Ariel said, smiling and waving good-bye. As she walked away, I heard her sneeze again.

One by one, the rest of my friends left. I lay back on my bed, feeling at peace. What a great day. A real Pocahontas day.

Chapter Four

Fur, Fur, Everywhere

Just before dinner I checked on Daisy again. She had drunk some water and eaten some fruit. I punched the air. "All right!" I whispered, trying not to startle her. She couldn't be too hurt if she was eating.

"How's our little patient?" asked Mom softly, coming out onto the screen porch.

"Okay so far," I said, pointing to the food and water dishes. "I've named her Daisy."

My mom frowned. "Now, don't get too attached to

her, honey. As soon as she's better, we're going to take her to the woods and release her back into her natural habitat."

"Whaaat?" I asked. "No way! We're going to keep her."

Mom shook her head. "No, ma'am. We have plenty of pets already. And armadillos aren't domesticated. She would be happier in the wild."

"But you said you thought she had been around dogs," I reminded Mom. "I bet she was someone's pet. Maybe she doesn't know how to survive in the wild."

"There's no way to tell until we try it," said Mom.

"Well, we have to keep her till she's better," I said firmly. "In the meantime, I'm going to look around for 'Lost Armadillo' signs, and see if her owner has missed her."

"Okay," Mom agreed. "We can keep her till she's better. And now it's time for you to give all our permanent pets their dinners."

"I'll be right there," I promised.

Hmm, maybe Mom has a point, I thought twenty minutes later. Everyone in my family takes turns feeding all our pets, and believe me, it's a big job. We actually have to keep a chart in the kitchen to keep track of everything.

For example, Duchess is seven years old. So she gets "senior" dog food. Jazzhot is only three, but he needs extra vitamins. Bobby will eat only grocery-store dog food, and then only the beef or lamb flavors. (My family and I are vegetarians. But we can't make our pets be vegetarians because it wouldn't be healthy for them. So we buy meat-based food for the ones who need it.)

Stopit and Nomore like dry kitty kibble. But Getdown likes canned food (only chicken or turkey flavors—no fish), and she needs to be fed up on top of our refrigerator because the other cats pick on her when she eats. (I don't know why.)

The four finches eat regular finch food, which is easy, but their cage is attached to a pulley on our dining room ceiling. To feed them you have to pull on the string and lower them to eye-level. We keep them up there because to our cats, the little birds just look like really fun, feathery cat toys.

Then there are Damon's saltwater fish. They're not plain goldfish. Oh, *no*. Actually what they are is miniature sharks. They're pygmy sharks that will never be longer than four or five inches. They're so cool and unique, but I don't want to talk about what they eat. Remember *Jaws?*

(My parents have never let me see that movie, but I've heard about it.)

Let's not forget Meeko. The Meekster is more work than all the other animals combined. He's the smartest, most adorable thing you've ever seen. When he sits on his fat haunches and gazes at me with his intelligent black eyes, and his little front paws are folded nicely on his soft, furry chest, my heart melts and I'm overwhelmed with love for him.

It almost makes me forget about the time he got into Dad's shoe polish. Or the peanut butter fiasco. Just last week there was the talcum powder incident, which took me an hour and a half to clean up. And Mom won't even buy pickles anymore. The living room still smells like them.

The deal is, raccoons are smart. They're very curious. And they have nimble little paws that can open things, like jars and cabinets and bottles of ketchup. So we put childproof locks on the refrigerator and the kitchen cabinets and even on the front and back doors, because Meeko had figured out how to open the doors and he would let all the other animals escape. I know it's only a matter of time before he figures out the child locks. And he's nocturnal, which means that he roams around at night doing his mischief while everyone is asleep and can't stop him.

With all our animals, our house always looks as if it could use a good vacuuming. During the spring, when the pets are shedding, it can be kind of overwhelming. We vacuum like every other day in the spring. Mom once said the cats were losing so much fur we almost had enough to mix it with paste and construct ourselves another cat. Taking good care of this many animals, four people, and our house is a lot of work.

Still, I couldn't help feeling that I wanted Daisy to be part of our family, too. She seemed so alone and defenseless, despite her hard, leathery shell. I liked the idea of having another unusual pet. Even though I had known her only a few hours, I cared about her. I didn't want to release her back into the wild.

Anyway, Mom had said Daisy could stay until she was all healed. I figured that by then, Mom would have fallen in love with her too. She would give in and say I didn't have to take Daisy back. Then we would have our own armadillo!

Later that night as I watched Daisy carefully venture

toward her dish of fruit, I felt my heart go out to her. Could it be that Daisy really was my animal spirit? Is that how people saw me—hard on the outside, soft on the inside? Quiet but strong? I would have to think more about this.

Chapter Five

Mermaids Like Fish Best

I could hardly wait to get home from school on Monday afternoon. (All of us except Jasmine take the school bus to and from Orlando Elementary. Because Jasmine lives in Wildwood Estates, her mom usually drives her.)

Today I practically leaped off the bus as soon as it came to my stop. Ariel trotted after me. (We have the same stop, since we live around the corner from each other.) We waved good-bye to Ella, Yukiko, and Isabelle, who would get off a couple stops farther on.

"Want to come over and see Daisy?" I asked Ariel as we walked quickly up the block.

"Sure," said Ariel. "Just remind me to call my mom and tell her where I am."

Both of us jumped up my front steps two at a time. I used my key to let us in, and found Mom studying at the dining room table. She waved her fingers at us and smiled, then turned her attention back to her books. She's had to learn so much stuff to be a vet. Tons of huge books. A couple of times she's stayed up all night studying. But soon she would take her exams, and then she would be Dr. Pinto.

First, Ariel and I grabbed a couple of bagels in the kitchen and Ariel called her mom.

"Where's the bad boy?" Ariel asked after she hung up. I knew who she meant.

"Meeko is asleep, of course," I told her. "Probably on top of the pecan sacks, in the basket on the back porch."

"With Daisy?" asked Ariel, taking a bite of bagel.

I shook my head. "Uh-uh. I moved Daisy inside to the bathroom after I did some research on the Internet. It said armadillos aren't that great at regulating their body temperature. I didn't want her to get chilled."

My house has one bathroom for all of us, and now an armadillo, too. I had set Daisy up in the bottom of our laundry hamper, which is a little cupboard with doors. We peeked in at her. Sure enough, she was sleeping, curled up on some old towels.

"Looks like she's back on a regular nocturnal schedule," I whispered.

"How's her paw?" Ariel asked softly. I had already told Ariel about how Mom had said I could keep Daisy only until she was well again.

"Mom says it's doing okay," I said. "Let's go to my room."

In my room I flopped down on my bed, and Ariel leaned back in my desk chair and propped her feet up on my desk. I used to have a beanbag chair, but the dogs took it over. After about a month of them sleeping in it, frankly I hadn't wanted it back.

"So, I've been looking for 'Lost Armadillo' signs, but I haven't found any yet," I told Ariel.

Ariel nodded and sneezed, which almost made her topple over.

"Do you still have that cold?" I asked. "Why did you even go to school today?"

"I *don't* have a cold!" Ariel said impatiently, wiping her nose with a tissue. "I was fine all yesterday, and today at school. I didn't sneeze once. It's only when I come *here* that I—" She stopped and her eyes widened.

"What?" I said. "You think it's something here?" Then it hit me. "Oh, no!" I cried. "You don't think—"

"Have I developed allergies?" Ariel gasped. "You know, my dad's allergic to everything. That's why we don't have any pets except fish. I didn't think I had any—I mean, I've been coming over here since I was five. But now, every time I step through the door I start sneezing!"

I thought for a moment. It couldn't be true. It was too horrible to be true. "Hold it," I said. "You were sneezing Saturday at the park. And we were outside."

"We were sitting on *your* blanket," Ariel reminded me. "It probably has some dog or cat fur on it."

"Probably?" I moaned. "Try definitely. I mean, Mom washed it just last week, but Nomore and Getdown were sleeping on it like the next day. And Meeko practically always gets on my bed."

For a few moments, Ariel and I looked at each other, horrified. Then Ariel sneezed again. Her eyes looked puffy and watery and red. I couldn't believe it. Could

Ariel have suddenly developed allergies to my pets? What would that mean? Ariel came over here like six times a week.

Maybe now my *best* best friend wouldn't even be able to come over to my house anymore! Maybe I'd always have to go to *her* house. Which wouldn't be so bad. It's just that Ariel has three sisters, and they're always around. It's hard to get privacy.

I didn't know what to say. Ariel sneezed again. Finally she got too miserable and sadly went home. I felt awful.

Chapter Six

Armadillos Are Way Cute

Before I went to bed that night, I visited Daisy in the bathroom. My brother, Damon, was in there brushing his teeth, but the door was open, so I went in.

"Hey," he said, his mouth dripping foam.

I grinned at him. "You look rabid."

He pretended to snarl at me, and I laughed.

Daisy was up on her hind legs, trying to look into the bathtub. Armadillos like water and are good swimmers. When her paw was better, I could fill the tub and let her play in it. That is, if Mom didn't make me get rid of her first.

"I helped Mom change her bandage earlier," Damon told me when he was done brushing his teeth. "Her paw looked good. But it might be harder for her to dig quickly with only three claws on that foot."

I nodded. "It might be harder for her to defend herself, too," I said. "Mom just has to change her mind!"

"Don't hold your breath," Damon advised, and left the bathroom.

I sat quietly and watched Daisy explore the bathroom. She waddled awkwardly, trying not to use her hurt paw, but she was curious and sniffed under the door and went over every inch of the floor. I gave her fresh water and cleaned up some food she had spilled. She was just so cool and interesting. Dogs and cats are terrific, of course, but an armadillo is unusual.

Is that why she might be my animal spirit? I wondered. Am I unusual? I frowned. My research on the Internet had told me that armadillos are real loners—the males and females stay apart almost all the time. Even the babies stay with their mother only for a while, then she shoos them away. That didn't sound like me. To tell you the truth, I had always thought of myself as more wolflike. Wolves are brave, strong, loyal, and very sociable. They

35

hang out with other wolves and form strong families. They cooperate and work together, but they can be independent, too. That felt more like me.

Still. I just loved little Daisy with her sniffy pink turtle nose.

I was sitting there, leaning my back against the bathtub, when I heard a muffled thump, a scrabbling noise, and then the sound of the doorknob turning. Guess who?

The door swung open and there was Meeko, hanging on to the doorknob like a fat, fuzzy oven mitt. He plopped down onto the tile floor, and I swung the door shut with my foot before any of the dogs could come in and make Daisy nervous.

Meeko walked cautiously over to Daisy and sniffed her, then sat back, folded his paws over his chest, and stared at me accusingly. Daisy seemed unimpressed with him, and went back to exploring. I laughed and picked Meeko up, cuddling him against my neck.

"You know I'll always love you best," I whispered. Meeko sniffed disdainfully and scrambled out of my arms. Pointy black nose twitching, he hurried over to Daisy's bowl of fruit and vegetables. He snatched up a chunk of apple, jumped from the edge of the bathtub up to the sink, turned on the cold water, and washed his apple. Then he sat back and munched it, seeming very pleased with himself. I couldn't help laughing.

"You think you're so smart," I teased him. He ate his apple smugly. That's how raccoons are. They can turn on water. They can open doors. They have no sense of right and wrong. It all boils down to: raccoons = trouble. But the Meekster is one of my best friends. He keeps secrets. I've cried into his fur. He makes me laugh. And he's completely adorable.

Daisy bumped my foot and I stroked her side gently. She ignored me and tried to open the bathroom door.

"I wish I could let you out," I told her. "But we have dogs and cats who might not like you as much as I do."

A tap on the door startled me. "Honey?" called my dad.

"Come on in," I said.

My dad stepped through the door and closed it behind him. "Okay, some of you have to go. I have to take out my contacts."

"Meeko and I will go," I said, scooping him into my arms. He smelled like apple. "Daisy will stay. Don't you think she's so, so cool, Dad?" I asked.

Dad looked at me as he opened his contact case. "We're

not keeping her, Paulish.* We've got too many animals already." He looked pointedly at Meeko, who snuggled into my shoulder. "We simply cannot have an armadillo in the house."

"But, Dad—" I began.

"But nothing," said Dad, waving his finger at me. "I'll tell you the same thing I told your mother: If one more animal comes into the house, I'm leaving. I'll go find myself a little room somewhere."

I rolled my eyes. I thought, I'm so sure. "Dad," I said patiently, "may I remind you that *you're* the one who brought home Duchess and Jazzhot because you felt sorry for them? *You're* the one who found Nomore in the parking lot at the bank and thought she looked hungry? And *you're* the one who brought home the Meekster." Meeko sniffed me and licked my cheek when he heard his name.

My dad filled his contact case with fluid. "That's beside the point," he said. "The fact remains that we are not keeping that armadillo, no matter how cute it is. I'm

(*We all have nicknames in my family. I'm Paulish. Damon is Damish. To us kids, Mom and Dad are sometimes Momish and Dadish. To each other, they're Willish and Jennish. I don't know how this all got started. It's pretty silly.)

38

drawing the line right here! So please don't make it harder on everyone by becoming attached to it."

Hmph, I thought, leaving the bathroom. He sounded pretty serious. In my mind, I pictured Daisy snuffling around our house, at home, safe and warm with us to take care of her. Tears almost came to my eyes. Despite everything Mom and Dad had said, I didn't know if I could bear to give her up.

Chapter Seven

I'm Making My Best Friend Sick!

"Yeah, so I went over to the bait shop, you know, the one right on the highway? I bought a box of mealworms for Daisy," I told my friends on Tuesday. "She loved them."

"Please," said Yukiko, making a face. "I'm trying to have my lunch here."

Ella, Yukiko, Jasmine, Isabelle, and I were at our usual table in the cafeteria. We always sit at the third table down from the window. I hadn't been on the school

40

bus—Mom had given me a ride to school—so I hadn't had a chance to talk with my friends.

"I have to admit, I felt guilty handing over the mealworms," I said, opening my container of macaroni salad.

"What mealworms?" Ariel said, plopping down her school lunch tray next to me. She slid into her seat.

"Hi! How do you feel?" I asked.

Ariel shrugged and flipped her long red hair over her shoulders. "Fine. No sneezing, no watery eyes, no— ah-choo! Ah-choo!"

We all stared at her. She pulled out a tissue and sneezed again. "I don't believe this!" she cried. "I was fine all last night and all this morning!"

"It's true," Ella said. "She didn't sneeze once on the bus."

"She wasn't sneezing in class, either," said Yukiko.

They looked at me, concerned. I got their meaning.

"You think it's *me*?" I cried. "You think I'm making Ariel sick?"

"Not on *purpose*," Isabelle said hastily.

Holding a tissue to her nose, Ariel looked me over. "Um, there," she said, sounding sniffly. She pointed at my sweater.

"Oh, no," I moaned, picking a single cat hair off. "This just came out of the dryer, and already it's contaminated!"

Sadly Ariel picked up her tray and switched places with Jasmine, down at the other end of the table. We tried to smile at each other, but we were miserable, and everyone could tell.

I put my head in my hands. "This is awful," I said. "First you can't even come over or sit on my blanket. Now you can't even sit next to me! I'm making my best friend sick!"

"It isn't you," said Ariel, sniffling. "It's just . . . something *about* you."

"How can we be best friends if we can't even sit next to each other?" I asked. I was getting majorly upset. I felt like I had the plague or something. "Are we just going to, like, talk on the *phone* all the time?"

"I don't know," Ariel whispered, looking down at her lunch. "I just don't know."

I pushed my salad away. The other Disney Girls looked at me sympathetically. "I need to ask Grandmother Willow what's going on," I said.

Yep, you heard right. I have my own Grandmother Willow, right in my backyard. Actually, my house is pretty small, but our backyard is huge. (One corner of it almost touches one corner of Ariel's yard, around the block.) We have three old willow trees, plus pecan trees, a live oak, and a row of sweet olive trees, too. (The sweet olives don't make olives. Just millions of tiny, cream-colored, sweet-smelling flowers.)

Anyway, Grandmother Willow is the biggest and oldest of all our trees. Her branches sweep down to the ground and make a secret, round room beneath them. The DGs and I hang out there all the time, especially in the summer. It's a magical place. I go to Grandmother Willow when I'm confused or need help.

Today after school I crawled beneath her branches. It felt cool and damp, and I lay on the ground feeling the chill seep through my clothes. The branches above were so thick I couldn't see the gray January sky.

I pulled my silver feather charm from under my sweater and held it in my hands. (Each of the Disney Girls has a magical charm. Mine is a silver feather. Ariel's is a gold seashell, of course. Jasmine has a tiny gold lamp on a chain. Isabelle has a small silver mirror. Yukiko wears a gold heart necklace. And Ella has a tiny, real crystal slipper. Our charms help remind us that magic is all around.)

Closing my eyes, I tried to relax and let magic come to me. Before I realized it, I was mumbling a special wish:

"All the magic powers that be,
Hear me now, my special plea.
Ariel's my *best* best friend.
Please let our friendship never end."

When I opened my eyes I felt a little calmer. I knew I had to believe that magic was on our side. With its help, we would be able to stay friends forever. In the meantime, what was with all the sneezing? Still holding my silver feather, I let my mind drift. I sent my thoughts out to Grandmother Willow and lay very still, awaiting her answer.

Then, like a tinkle of music heard on a breeze, her words of wisdom came to me. *Friends are friends from the heart. If you can get past what's outside, you will always be friends.*

Hmm. I sat up and pondered that for a while. It sort of sounded like "You can't judge a book by its cover," but that couldn't be it. I shook my head. Sometimes I have to think about Grandmother Willow's advice for a couple of days before it makes sense.

As I crawled out from under the tree, I felt better. I knew that Ariel and I would always be in tight with each other, even if we could only talk on the phone. We were Disney Girls. We were *best* best friends. Our hearts would stay together, even if the rest of us couldn't be in the same room.

Chapter Eight

Needed:
Good Home for Armadillo

By Wednesday morning my feeling better had completely gone to poofville. (You know—*poof*! It's gone.) I dragged myself to the school bus stop and barely made it on time. Ariel was there waiting, and we smiled sadly at each other, but I kept my distance. On the bus, I sat next to Yukiko. Ariel and I didn't even try to sit together anymore.

"Pretty down, huh?" Yukiko asked.

I nodded. "Mom says Daisy's paw is healed well enough for her to be released. If I can't find her a good home by Saturday, it's back to the woods."

"That's too bad," said Ella, turning around in her seat to talk. "But I bet Daisy would be a good pet. Have you started asking around?"

"Uh-uh," I said. An idea popped into my mind. "Hey!" I said, looking at my friends. "How about if one of you—"

"Don't even go there," Yukiko said regretfully. "I've got six brothers, one sister, four cats, and some fish. Mom and Jim would croak if I brought home an armadillo."

From three seats away, Ariel said, "Armadillos do have some fur, so I don't think Dad could have her in the house. Anyway, if she lived with me, you would never see her."

I made a face. It was true. Not only could Ariel not come to my house, but now I couldn't even go to her house. Even when I wore perfectly clean clothes right out of the dryer, just being next to Ariel made her sneeze. It was a big rain cloud in my life, let me tell you. Our bus pulled up to Orlando Elementary, and we piled out. Jasmine was waiting for us, as usual. I asked her if she thought she could adopt Daisy.

"Count me out," Jasmine said, looking sorry. "My mom hasn't even gotten used to Rajah yet.

47

Plus, an armadillo would totally clash with her furniture."

I almost smiled. Rajah is Jasmine's orange tabby kitten. He gets into almost as much mischief as Meeko. Well, maybe half as much, which is still a lot. And Jasmine's mom, Mrs. Prentiss, is really nice, but they live in a huge, fancy mansion and she gets nervous about keeping it all looking perfect.

"You know, we already have two dogs," said Isabelle. "But I don't think also having an armadillo would be that big a deal. I'll ask Mom and Dad."

"Really?" I cried. "Awesome! Thanks, Isabelle."

"I'll ask Dad and Alana, too," said Ella. (Alana is her stepmother. Ella is Cinderella, and she has a stepmother and two stepsisters. But they're not wicked or anything. I think they all get along okay now.) "We already have two cats and two mice, but it can't hurt to ask."

"Thank you guys so much," I said, breathing a sigh of relief. "If Daisy could live with one of you, it would be almost as good as keeping her myself."

Kids streamed past us, going in to school, and in a few minutes the bell rang. All during the day I kept thinking and thinking about what to do with Daisy.

"Bad news," Isabelle said later that night. She had called me after dinner. "Mom and Dad said no to Daisy. They think we've got our hands full with Snuffles and Pokey."

"But she wouldn't be any trouble," I argued.

"I know," Isabelle sighed. "They just don't want the hassle. I really tried."

I bit my lip. "I know. I appreciate it. But Ella's parents said no, too. And Mom says Daisy has to be gone by Saturday. I don't know what to do."

"Would a pet shop take her?" Isabelle suggested.

"No," I said. "She's not domesticated. Besides, I wouldn't want her to be sold to some stranger who might not take care of her."

"Well, I'm sorry," said Isabelle. "I really wish I could take her. You'll figure out something."

I hope so, I thought as we hung up the phone. I sure hope so.

"Absolutely not," my mom said in her most no-nonsense voice.

"But, Mom," I pleaded. "No one else can take her!"

"Honey, she doesn't *need* to be taken by anyone," my

49

mom said. "She'll do fine on her own in the woods. Look, on Saturday morning we'll drive her over by Puzzle Lake. It's beautiful around there. The ground is soft for digging holes, there's plenty of stuff for her to eat, there's water right there . . . it's an armadillo's paradise."

I crossed my arms over my chest and looked at the floor. It *sounded* good, but I wasn't convinced. Daisy seemed happy right where she was—with me. She had been on her own before, and look what happened. She'd gotten hurt, she'd gone hungry, she'd gotten lost and confused. I couldn't bear not knowing what happened to her after she waddled away from us in the woods. I couldn't stand wondering if she was okay, or if she had gotten hurt again. Just thinking about it made my throat hurt. I wiped the back of my hand across my eyes.

"Look, sweetie," my mom said gently, patting my back. "I know how you feel about animals. I feel the same way. And Daisy is a sweet little thing. But you know we can't keep every animal we find. And you also know that it isn't a good idea to try to keep wild animals as house pets. It isn't fair to us or to them. Of course we'll miss Daisy, but believe me, she'll be happier out in the woods, digging up grubs and termites."

Part of me knew Mom was right. But part of me hated to admit it. And *all* of me didn't want to send Daisy back into the wild. I had to find another solution. And I had forty-eight hours to find it.

Chapter Nine

Armadillo Incognito

1) Harry's Wild Animal Park
2) Gatorworld
3) University of Florida, Animal Science
   Department
4) Animal Shelter of Orlando

"Wow," said Jasmine, reading my list on Friday morning. "You've tried everything I could think of."

"Maybe you could put an ad in the paper," Ella suggested.

I sighed and swung my feet against the bench. My buds

and I were hanging out in the playground before the bell rang to start class. I had spent yesterday afternoon on the phone, calling places that might possibly want an armadillo. No one had wanted Daisy.

Now the six of us were scorching our brain cells, trying to find Daisy a home.

"Hey, guys," called a voice. "Why the miserable faces? Oh, sorry. I forgot you were born that way."

I looked up and groaned silently. The Beast—Kenny McIlhenny—was walking toward us. Before I had met Isabelle, Kenny McIlhenny had been just another APB— Annoying Pesty Boy. But when we realized Isabelle was really Belle, we found out that she came with her very own Beast: Kenny. They live right next door to each other, and have been enemies since they were babies.

"Keep hiking, Kenny," Isabelle said, jerking her thumb over her shoulder.

"No, seriously, you guys seem down," Kenny said, trying to look concerned and only looking sneaky.

"It's none of your bus—" I began.

"We need to find a home for Paula's armadillo!" Ella blurted. I glared at her, and she blushed.

"Really?" Kenny asked, sounding interested. "An

armadillo, huh? Cool. Tell you what: I'll take it. I've always wanted an armadillo."

"Oh, really?" I said, giving him the ice look.

"Yeah!" His face lit up. "I hear they're great barbecued! Ha ha ha!" Laughing hard, he sauntered off.

Isabelle shook her head disgustedly. "I swear, if I could find *his* magic rose, I would throw it to the ground and stomp it to bits."

I couldn't help smiling.

"Okay," said Ariel, clapping her hands. (She was sitting as far away from me as she could.) "Let's get serious. Paula's tried all the normal places for Daisy to live. How about weird places—like Willow Green?"

I shook my head. "I thought of that. I'm afraid dogs would chase her, or she'd wander into the street and get hit by a car again."

"The state park?" said Yukiko.

"The thing is, I just can't stand the thought of releasing her into the wild," I said. "I have to be able to find her and check up on her. If I take her to the state park, or the woods, or anywhere like that, I'll never see her again."

The bell rang for school to begin, and we stood up. I didn't know how I would get through this whole school day knowing that by tomorrow morning, Mom would be loading Daisy into the cat carrier. I started to mope my way to class. It makes me crazy when I can't fix things or solve problems. I like taking action—getting things done.

"Okay, okay," said Ariel, waving her hands. "I give in. I can't stand to see you like this. I'll hide Daisy in my room until you find a better place, okay? So I'll sneeze a little. What's a runny nose between friends?"

I turned to smile at her. That's one of the best things about having great friends like the DGs. They would do anything for me. Chuckling, I pictured Ariel hiding Daisy in her room. After all, Daisy would sleep all day. . . .

I froze.

Jasmine bumped into me. All the kids on their way to class split around us and passed us by.

"What's the matter, Paula?" Yukiko asked.

I put my hands to my cheeks. "Oh, my gosh!" I said. "Oh, my gosh! Ariel, you're brilliant!"

"Naturally," said Ariel, tossing her red hair over her shoulder. "But why am I brilliant *this* time?"

"Look, I know I can't keep Daisy forever," I said quickly. "But I need more time to find her a good home.

In the meantime, I have to keep her warm and safe. And where's a warm, safe place? *My room!* You were right when you said we could hide her. But instead of your room, I'll hide her in *my* room! I'll keep looking for a good place for her to live, and when I find one, I'll sneak her out. Mom and Dad will never know! How can I thank you?"

I threw my arms around Ariel. One second later, she started sneezing.

"Um, you can thank me by wrapping yourself in plastic," Ariel said, sneezing again and pushing me off her.

"Sorry," I said, dancing away till there was a good six feet between us. "Sorry. But thank you, thank you, thank you!"

Chapter Ten

Operation Daisy

"I know you feel bad about it, honey," said my mom.
"But you're doing the right thing."

The night before, the other DGs and I had talked on
the phone for ages, working out the details of my plan.
This morning, Saturday, I had woken early, ready to put
it into action.

Now I eased Daisy into our cat carrier and latched the
door. Since it was daytime, Daisy was groggy, and settled
down on her towel right away. I stroked her nose through
the mesh, and tried not to meet Mom's eyes.

"Yeah, I guess you're right," I said. "Isabelle, do you have the bus map?"

Isabelle waved the map. She didn't look at my mom either. Usually Ariel would be helping me—she's always up for an adventure. But since she couldn't come to my house or even get near me, Isabelle had agreed to be my partner in Operation Daisy. "Just don't ask me to lie to your parents," she had begged. I had agreed to make sure she didn't need to.

I stood up, slung my backpack on over my jeans jacket, and hefted the carrier. Daisy was heavier than any of our cats, and it took both hands.

"Are you sure you can manage that?" Mom asked. "You don't want me to give you a ride to the Nature Center?"

"Nah, that's okay," I said. "Isabelle will help me. We have to change buses only once, and I won't have to carry her very far."

Were my cheeks burning? It felt like it. I hated tricking Mom this way. But I was desperate, and I didn't see any other solution. I had to do what was best for Daisy.

"Okay, sweetie," said Mom. She leaned over and kissed my cheek. I felt terrible. I managed a weak smile, then Isabelle and I got out of the house as fast as we could.

"Whew," said Isabelle as we headed down my walk, our backs stick-straight. "That was a bummer."

We turned left. I was dying to look back to see if Mom was watching, but I didn't dare. Isabelle and I were going to walk around the corner to "go catch the bus." Actually, we were going to Ariel's house. It was all part of the plan.

"Tell me about it," I agreed. "Usually I tell Mom everything. But she just doesn't understand how tight I am with Daisy."

Speaking of Daisy, she was getting heavier with every step I took. I was glad I wasn't really lugging her across town to the Orlando Nature Center (who had turned Daisy down, BTW).

Ariel was waiting for us on her front porch. "Everything go okay?" she called softly.

Slipping behind the cypress tree in her front yard, I gave her a thumbs-up. "Coast clear?"

She took a good look around, then nodded and waved us down the driveway to her backyard. Ariel has a nice backyard, but it's smaller than ours because her house is bigger.

Isabelle and I sneaked toward the back, crouching low and keeping close to the row of crape myrtle trees.

Halfway down the driveway, Ella was crouched behind the azalea bushes. "Hi, guys!" she whispered. "So far, so good. Wait till Yukiko gives you the sign before you cut across the back."

Isabelle and I nodded. We reached the end of the crape myrtle trees and sank to our knees. It felt good to put Daisy down for a minute. In the backyard, Yukiko and Jasmine were rocking slowly in Mrs. Ramos's glider. From where they sat, they could see the entire back of Ariel's house, and most of the backyard.

I caught Yukiko's eye. She barely held up one finger, signaling me to wait a minute. Isabelle and I held our breaths. Then Yukiko shot us a little thumbs-up.

"Now!" I whispered.

Hunching low, Isabelle and I scurried across Ariel's backyard as fast as we could. When we finally reached the bamboo thicket at the edge of the yard, my heart was pounding. My hands were cramped from carrying Daisy. I checked behind us. All was clear.

"Jeez," breathed Isabelle. "I would make a lousy spy. This is killing me. I guess I'm not a sneaky cat after all."

"Me, too." I took off my backpack. Unzipping it, I pulled out a black hooded sweatshirt, which I put on.

Isabelle turned her windbreaker inside out—it was navy blue inside. I had thought about putting camouflage paint on my face, but had decided it'd be too hard to get off.

"Okay," I said almost silently. "Now for phase two."

Phase one had taken us out of my house and through Ariel's backyard. Now we were in the neutral zone between our houses. Last year, Ariel and I had discovered a secret passage from her yard to mine. We use it only in emergencies. This counted as one.

Once Isabelle and I were ready, we linked pinkies for good luck. Then I pulled my hood up, gripped the cat carrier, and pushed through the thick bamboo. On the other side was a fig tree, which we climbed, handing Daisy's carrier back and forth. From the tree, we lowered ourselves to the metal shed roof of Ariel's neighbor. We crossed the roof, trying to be fast and silent and safe all at the same time. It was only about a six foot drop to the ground, but still, I felt as if I could hardly breathe. Finally I was able to drop to the ground behind the shed. Isabelle handed Daisy to me and scrambled down herself.

Behind the shed, we rested before phase three. I smiled nervously at Isabelle. Her eyes looked wide and dark. I didn't think she was enjoying herself. It made me miss Ariel so much. She would have been loving this.

"Ready?" I asked.

Isabelle nodded and took a deep breath. I picked up Daisy again. We left the tiny alley, pushed through some banana trees, and hopped a low fence. *Voila.* We were in my backyard.

Isabelle positioned herself beneath Grandmother Willow, with just her head barely poking out from the feathery leaves. I slithered from tree to bush to tree to the potting bench, checking with Isabelle every time to make sure I was okay.

Behind the potting bench, I hunkered down and waited for Isabelle's signal. Finally I heard it—a low whistle. Trying not to quake with fear, I grabbed Daisy's carrier and ran lightly up the back steps to my own house. I eased open the back door and paused, listening. It sounded like Mom was still in the kitchen. I ducked through the family room and down the hall, past the bathroom to my room.

I had prepared my closet the night before. Daisy's cozy blanket was there, as was a small bowl of water and some cut-up vegetables. Working fast, I opened Daisy's carrier.

She was sleepy and didn't want to leave it. I finally had to tip her out. She tumbled onto her blanket, her claws raking the plastic carrier. I shoved my closet door closed, and slunk out of the house as quietly as I had slunk in.

Then I raced down the back steps toward Isabelle, moving silently from tree to tree again, staying in the shadows, keeping low. At last I threw myself under Grandmother Willow's sheltering branches and lay on the chilly ground, panting.

"Mission accomplished?" Isabelle asked worriedly.

I nodded. "Operation Daisy was successful—at least for now."

Chapter Eleven

The Sniffles Mystery

I thought I would feel majorly relieved after Daisy was hidden in my closet. After all, now I wouldn't have to worry about her being alone in the woods. But actually, that worry was replaced by a whole new concern: What if my parents found her?

Isabelle and I sat up.

"I guess we need to kill some time," I said. "To make it look like we went to the Nature Center and back, by bus."

"Uh-huh," said Isabelle. "I have to tell you, you can't go home looking like that."

Glancing down, I saw that Isabelle was right. My clothes were covered with dirt, rust from the fence, banana-tree juice, and grass stains. I had leaves in my hair and dirt under my fingernails.

"Okay," I decided. "Let's go back to Ariel's. I'll wash my clothes there."

We snuck back through the secret passage. It was much easier this time, since the cat carrier was empty. Ariel let us in as soon as we knocked on her back door. She ran upstairs to get me some spare clothes, and I quickly changed in the downstairs bathroom.

Ten minutes later, the six DGs were drinking hot chocolate and eating popcorn in the Ramoses' kitchen. I started to feel more cheerful. All of a sudden I noticed something.

"Hey," I said to Ariel. "You're not sneezing."

"No duh," she said. "You're wearing my clothes, in my house. There's no dog or cat hair anywhere." Her face brightened. "I guess this means you can come over to hang out, as long as you change into my clothes! All *right*!"

I smiled, too. "You can keep a stash of Paula clothes right by the front door."

"You know, guys," said Isabelle, "I'm sitting right here next to Ariel. She's not sneezing. But I have two dogs. I'm sure I must have some kind of dog hair on me somewhere."

Ariel leaned over and peered at Isabelle's thermal shirt. She plucked a short gray hair off it. "Yeah, this looks like Pokey's hair, all right." Putting her face right next to Isabelle's shoulder, Ariel inhaled deeply. We all waited on pins and needles.

No sneeze. Not even a nose twitch.

Jasmine, on Ariel's other side, held up a finger. "What about me? Rajah actually slept on this shirt, because I forgot to put my laundry away. I've been feeling like a big walking furball all day. But Ariel isn't sneezing."

For a few minutes we sat there, trying to get our brain cells to connect. On one hand, right now Ariel didn't seem to be allergic to dog or cat fur. On the other hand, she still sneezed when she came over to my house. Or even when she got close to me.

I gasped and put my hands over my mouth. "You're allergic to *me*!" I wailed. "You're actually allergic to me, myself!"

Ariel's green eyes opened wide in alarm. My heart felt

like it dropped down into my knees. How could my *best* best friend be allergic to me! It was impossible!

Then Ariel's face relaxed. "Look, Paula, you're sitting right here. I'm not sneezing. It isn't *you*."

"It's something on your clothes," said Yukiko.

"But what?" asked Ella. "If it isn't animal fur—"

"Maybe bird feathers from the finches?" said Jasmine.

"Your shampoo," said Isabelle.

"Something you ate?" suggested Ariel.

I made a face. "How could something I *ate* make you sneeze?"

"I don't know!" Ariel said, throwing up her hands. "I can't figure this out!"

Sighing, I stood up and got my own clothes out of the dryer. I held them out and Ariel sniffed them. Nothing. She patted my shoulder. "It's a mystery," she said. "But we'll figure it out. I mean, we're going to be best friends for another seventy years, at least. We'll work something out so we can hang together."

I nodded, thinking, I sure hope so.

Back home, Mom asked me how it had gone at the Nature Center. I felt as if I had GUILTY written on my forehead in big red letters. "Um, fine," I said, and quickly disappeared to my room.

It took me two seconds to whip open my closet door and peek in at Daisy. She was curled up asleep on her favorite blankie. I was so happy to see her. And look how quiet and good she was being. Mom and Dad would never suspect a thing. All I had to do now was work hard to find Daisy a place that I was happy about. I was sure I could do it—I just needed more time. It was a huge comfort to know that Daisy would be warm and safe while I looked.

I shut the closet door and flopped down on my bed. Right now I had two big goals: to find Daisy a new home, and to figure out the mystery of Ariel's sniffles. What would Pocahontas do? Where should I begin?

Chapter Twelve

Magic's Mysterious Answer

Pocahontas's Journal

Monday

So far, so good with Daisy, but I don't know how long I can keep her hidden. The dogs keep sniffing around my closet door, and this morning Bobby was actually trying to pull the door open! Damon saw me shooing Bobby away, and he said, "Maybe it's time you washed your gym socks." Very funny. This afternoon I called five pet shops, but no one wants Daisy. I don't like that idea anyway— what if someone bought her who doesn't know how to take care of her? I want to be able to *see* where she's going to live. I'm running out of ideas.

Tuesday

Today I couldn't walk down the hall with Ariel at school. She started sneezing too much. *What is going on?* We talk every day on the phone, but still. We always used to hang together. I miss her so much! During math today I was reading an armadillo book under my desk. Mr. Murchison called on me and I didn't know the answer. I feel so worried about Daisy and so upset about Ariel I can hardly pay attention in school. This isn't like me. I have to chill out.

Wednesday

Yesterday I called every animal services place I could find in the phone book. They all told me armadillos don't make good pets, and that I should release her into the wild. Have I been wrong about Daisy? Every time I look at her little face, her pointy pink nose, I think I'm doing the right thing. She's so sweet! How could anyone not want her? I even put up a sign on the bulletin board at the OE library, but no one has called. (I used Ariel's phone number.)

On top of everything, I have to keep Meeko out on the screen porch all the time, because he opened my closet door a couple times. So he's really mad at me. He's acting like I don't love him anymore. Of course I do! It's just that Daisy needs me right now. Anyway, the Meekster is being Mr. Obnoxious. He opened Mom's bag of potting soil and made a huge mess. He chewed on the porch swing, which Dad was mad about. And he keeps tapping on the glass door at night, which makes the dogs bark, which upsets the cats, which upsets Mom and Dad. . . . Sometimes that raccoon makes me crazy. *He's* the one I should take out to the woods!

Thursday

My life is getting worse by the day. Where is my magic? Today I totally forgot a science quiz. Luckily, I knew a lot of it anyway, but I like to do my best on tests.

My head is all fogged up because I haven't been getting enough sleep. The dogs' barking (thanks to you-know-who) keeps me up, and so does Daisy. I let her out of the closet at night so she can stretch her legs. She makes so much noise exploring that it's hard for me to sleep. Last night she tried to *dig* her way out of my room! She knocked over my little bottle of pretty sand, and the edge chipped. She really needs to be outside—it's majorly hard cleaning up after her. What am I going to do?

Friday

Today I broke down and begged magic to help get me out of this mess. This afternoon, I rushed home from school to check on Daisy. I found Mom about to open my closet door to put some laundry away! I shrieked, "Wait!" Mom stared at me like I was bananas. "Um," I said. "I mean, you don't have to do that. I'll put it away." I smiled, feeling like such a faker. "You have enough to do already." Mom's dark eyes narrowed thoughtfully. I swallowed hard. Mom has a way of looking at me as if she was seeing all the way through to my soul.

Without saying a word, she handed me the clothes and quietly left the room. I felt *sooo* bad. Not telling Mom and Dad the truth makes me feel terrible. I don't like being dishonest. I think it makes my magic dull and weak.

Anyway. After Mom left, I checked on Daisy. She was fine. Then I raced outside to Grandmother Willow. I scrambled beneath the branches and threw my arms around her trunk. Everything got to me all at once and the tears ran out of my eyes like rain. I cried for a long time.

Finally, I calmed down, closed my eyes, and tried to concentrate. I could hardly feel any tingle of magic at all. Still, I squeezed my silver feather hard and tried to exhale deeply, breathing out all my confusion and breathing in magic and light. I whispered:

"All the magic powers that be,
Hear me now, my desperate plea.
My world right now is falling down.
Where can Daisy's home be found?"

Then I sat very still, my hands on my knees. Thoughts were swirling through my head like autumn leaves on a breeze. But slowly my mind cleared, and I felt the warmth of magic caress my face. I felt Grandmother Willow's answer float gently into my mind: *Daisy belongs to magic, as magic belongs to you.*

Frowning, I concentrated harder, hoping for more info—something more specific. Nothing else came, and finally I opened my eyes. "Daisy belongs to magic, as magic belongs to me?" I whispered. "What the heck does that mean?"

I need to go now—Mom is calling me for dinner. There's only one thing to do: I have to call an emergency meeting of the Disney Girls.

Chapter Thirteen

The Breaking Point

"Okay, the first item on the agenda is some thinking food," said Ella briskly. I smiled. Even at nine o'clock on a Saturday morning, Ella was totally organized, as usual. Thank goodness for the Disney Girls—they had come through for me again. Half an hour after I called them, we had gathered in Ella's big, sunny kitchen.

For most of her life, Ella had lived with her dad in a small apartment at the edge of Willow Hill. But when Mr. O'Connor got remarried last July, he and Ella moved with his new wife and her two daughters to this big Victorian house much closer to the rest of us DGs. It's a neat house, and Ella's room is majorly cool—it has a real turret.

"What kind of thinking food?" Isabelle asked.

"How about chocolate/banana/yogurt smoothies?" Ella said, gathering the ingredients.

"Yum," I said, sliding onto a kitchen stool. "Thanks for coming, you guys. I have to solve the Daisy situation ASAP, before I lose my mind."

"Here," Jasmine said, handing the bananas to Ella. "Yeah, Paula, you've been looking kind of stressed all week. But what can we do? You've already done everything we could think of."

I sighed in frustration. "I know. But there must be something we're *not* thinking of."

As Ella sliced the bananas into big chunks, one of her stepmother's Siamese cats jumped up on the counter. He nosed around her hand, and she tried to shoo him away.

Ariel giggled and petted him. "What's he doing?"

"Vlad loves bananas," Ella sighed. She put some small chunks into a dish on the floor. Vlad leaped down and fell on them, purring as he ate.

"Weird," said Ariel.

A thought hit me. "Ariel, you were petting Vlad!" I said.

"Yeah, so?" Ariel looked mystified.

"You weren't sneezing!" I said. "If it isn't dogs and isn't cats, then you really *must* be allergic to *me*." I felt more depressed than ever.

Just then, Ms. Rogers (Ella's stepmom) came in with two bags of groceries. "Hi, girls," she said, smiling.

"Are there more groceries outside?" asked Ella.

"No, honey, this is it," said Ms. Rogers. She set the bags down on the kitchen counter next to Ariel. "Whew! That store was crowded."

"Ah-choo!" Ariel grabbed a tissue and held it to her nose. "Ah-choo! Ah-choo!"

We all stared at Ariel, wondering what had set her off. I was a good six feet away from her.

"Ah-choo!"

Isabelle's eyes opened wide. "Oh, my gosh!" Quickly she pulled the grocery bag closer to her and started pawing through the contents. One by one she waved items under Ariel's nose. Cheese? No. Paper towels? No. Window cleaner? No.

"What are you doing?" asked Yukiko.

"Something in this bag is making Ariel sneeze!" Isabelle said.

Ariel leaned over and inhaled deeply as Isabelle held a tube of toothpaste under her nose. "Nope, that's not it," she said.

Isabelle dug in the bag and pulled out a box of fabric softener sheets. As soon as she held them up, Ariel started sneezing so much she almost fell over.

"This is it!" Isabelle said, holding them up. "Ariel's allergic to this!"

"That's a new brand that the store was promoting," said Ms. Rogers. "But if they make Ariel sneeze, I won't use them."

I sniffed the box too. They smelled familiar—because my mom had been using them, too! The mystery was solved!

Ariel kept sneezing. She waved at Isabelle to put the box away. Ms. Rogers took the box and sealed it inside a plastic bag. Almost immediately, Ariel's sneezing fit stopped. Ms. Rogers smiled at her, then went upstairs.

"I can't believe it!" I said. "You're not allergic to dogs or cats or *me*. You're allergic to my dryer sheets!"

"That's why I didn't sneeze when you wore my clothes," said Ariel, sniffling. She and I looked at each other happily.

"Yay, Detective Isabelle!" said Jasmine.

Isabelle bowed. "Thank you, thank you."

"I'll ask Mom to quit using those sheets right away," I said. "Now we can hang tight again!" I felt as if the sun had just come out.

"Okay," said Ella. She handed us each a smoothie. It was delicious. "We skipped ahead to item two on the agenda, but that's okay. I'm glad the Ariel thing is solved. Now we can fix item one."

My face fell again as I remembered poor little Daisy. "You know, guys, I asked Grandmother Willow what to do about Daisy. For once, she didn't help me that much. She said that Daisy belongs to magic, like magic belongs to us. I don't understand what that means."

"Hmm," Ariel said, tapping her chin.

"Daisy belongs to magic?" repeated Yukiko.

"And magic belongs to us," said Jasmine, frowning.

"Okay, let's think," said Ella. "Daisy belongs to magic. Magic belongs to us." She leaned her chin on her hand and looked off into space.

"Magic, magic, magic," Ariel muttered.

"Well, what does magic mean to us?" asked Isabelle, holding out her arms. "Where does it come from?"

I closed my eyes and pondered. Magic comes from . . .
well, everything, I thought. It comes from connections—
to each other, to the earth, to all of nature. . . .

My eyes snapped open. "Oh, jeez," I gasped. "My mom
was right!"

Chapter Fourteen

Daisy's Magical Home

"Look," I explained eagerly as my friends gathered around me. "Where does our magic come from? From each other, from nature, from everything around us, right? We just open ourselves to magic, and it flows to us."

"Okay, I'm following you," said Jasmine. "But how does Daisy fit into it?"

"Grandmother Willow was telling me that Daisy belongs to nature," I concluded. "Just like nature belongs to us. And to all living things on the planet."

"Whoa," whispered Ariel. "Heavy."

"So when Mom told me to release Daisy back into the wild, she was right," I continued. "I was thinking of the woods as the place Daisy got lost and hurt. But she was lost in *our neighborhood.* Not in the woods. In the woods is where she feels at home. When Daisy's surrounded by nature, she's surrounded by magic. And magic will help protect her and take care of her."

I beamed at my friends, feeling like Einstein.

Yukiko shook her head. "You are so, so brilliant," she said softly.

"This is amazing," Jasmine agreed.

Grinning at the Disney Girls, I said, "Time for Operation Daisy—part two."

Mrs. Ramos agreed to drive us and Daisy all out to Puzzle Lake, which is where my mom had wanted to take Daisy in the first place. The Disney Girls quickly made plans: we would do Operation Daisy again, but in reverse. This time we would sneak Daisy *out* of my house, instead of in.

"Okay, my mom is home right now because she just finished taking all her vet exams," I briefed my friends.

"How'd she do?" asked Ariel.

"I don't know," I said. "I hope okay. Anyway, let's wait until she goes into the kitchen. Then I'll run in through the back, put Daisy in the cat carrier, and run back out. We'll sneak her down the driveway and around the corner."

"My mom will be waiting in the minivan," Ariel said.

"Okay." I met each of my friend's eyes. If we could pull this off, my life would be back to normal by tonight. Ariel and I could hang out again, Daisy would be happy in her new home, and I would no longer have to keep a secret from my parents. I would be in heaven.

It all went like clockwork. I was getting to be an old hand at this sneaking around stuff. As soon as Jasmine gave me the signal, I raced in, coaxed a sleepy Daisy into the carrier, and padded silently out the back door. Then I started to slink down the driveway. I had forgotten how heavy Daisy was.

Suddenly I heard the sound of a window opening above me. I froze, hoping I was invisible against the trees. My mom stuck her head out the window. I shoved the carrier in back of me and plastered an innocent expression on my face.

"Have you finally found a home for that armadillo?" Mom asked.

My mouth dropped open. "Wha—?" I sputtered. "Uh, what armadillo?" That's me. A quick thinker, for sure.

"Oh, please," Mom said, rolling her eyes. "You must think I was born yesterday. If someone hides an armadillo in my house, I'm going to know about it."

"Uh, uh . . ." I stammered, my brain whirling furiously.

"I mean, a big clue was when your father woke up to find an armadillo trying to burrow under the covers with him," Mom went on.

I gasped in horror. When had that happened?

"Yes, as slow as we old fogeys are, we managed to put two and two together, after that." Mom crossed her arms over her chest and looked at me wryly.

My face was burning. I was so, so embarrassed. I didn't know what to say.

"Now, where are you taking her?" Mom asked.

"Puzzle Lake," I muttered, hanging my head.

Mom was silent for a few moments. "I think that would be best," she said gently. "You've made the right decision. I'm sure of it."

I nodded. "I'm sure, too."

Mom smiled and started to close the window.

"Oh, Mom?" I called back. She paused, and I smiled sheepishly at her. "Thanks," I said. Mom winked at me, then closed the window.

I ran down the driveway, humming.

Of course Daisy totally loved her new home. I was worried that she would refuse to come out of her carrier. Or worse, that she would stand there and gaze at me accusingly, like Meeko does whenever things don't go his way. But I didn't have to worry.

As soon as we got to Puzzle Lake, the Disney Girls and I walked away from the car about two hundred yards into the woods. It was an armadillo's paradise, just like Mom said. I opened the carrier and held my breath. Daisy immediately poked her nose out and sniffed the air. In seconds she had waddled out of the carrier and shuffled toward a thicket. She didn't even look back. Thirty seconds later, I couldn't see or hear her anymore. Daisy was out of my life forever.

I felt my throat close up and my eyes start watering. "Bye, Daisy," I whispered.

Ariel put her arm around me, but started sneezing.

(I didn't have any clothes that hadn't been dried with those dryer sheets.) She moved away again.

Jasmine came and put her arm around me, and Ella patted my back.

"She's really happy now," Ella told me. "She wasn't supposed to be a pet."

I nodded and wiped my eyes. "I guess you're right."

"Hey—I have an idea," said Isabelle. She pulled her silver mirror charm out from under her sweater. "Let's see if we can find Daisy. If we can, then we can check up on her every once in a while."

"Great!" I cried. The six of us linked pinkies and closed our eyes. We chanted:

"All the magic powers that be,
Hear us now, our special plea.
In love with Daisy we all fell,
Please show us that she's doing well."

Then we opened our eyes and peered into Isabelle's tiny mirror. At first it was foggy, as usual. Gradually it cleared, and in the tiny reflection I saw Daisy! She was already digging a cozy new home for herself in a sandy bank beneath a huge fallen log. Her three-toed front paw didn't seem to be slowing her down a bit. I got all choked up again, this time from happiness. Magic was everywhere. And it would help take care of Daisy.

"Group hug, group hug!" Ella said.

I groaned. Total cornville. But the six of us scrambled close together and squeezed as hard as we could.

"Ah-choo!"

Here's a sneak preview of
DisneyGirls

#7 Adventure at Walt Disney World . . .

The thing about magic is that you have to remember to let it do its stuff. I mean, you just have to trust magic to do what's best, even if at first it doesn't seem like what you wanted at all. So when the six of us wished for the best spring vacation ever, we had no idea what to expect.

"Don't forget—my ninth birthday is coming up," I told my friends. We were sitting downstairs in my family room, eating popcorn and waiting for our video to rewind. I had finally agreed to host another DG sleepover (even though I hadn't totally recovered from my disastrous first sleepover).

"No-duh," said Ariel, tossing some popcorn into her mouth.

"Are you going to have a party, Isabelle?" asked Paula. "Should we plan something special ourselves?"

"Yeah—" I began, then my dad came downstairs.

"Speaking of birthdays," he said, smiling at us, "your mother and I have a special birthday surprise for you."

"Really?" I sat up eagerly.

"Yep," he said proudly. "Six week-long passes to the Disney Institute at Walt Disney World. One for you and each of your friends."

For several moments there was complete silence. Then I jumped up and screamed. I threw my arms around my dad just as Mom came in.

"Disney World!" I shrieked. "A week at the Disney Institute! Oh, my gosh!" I jumped up and down and squealed some more. I probably looked like a total dweeb, but I didn't care. The biggest wish of my life had just come true—for me and my friends.

Read all the books in the
Disney Girls series!

#1 *One of Us*

Jasmine is thrilled to be a Disney Girl. It means she has four best friends—Ariel, Yukiko, Paula, and Ella. But she still doesn't have a *best* best friend. Then she meets Isabelle Beaumont, the new girl. Maybe Isabelle could be Jasmine's *best* best friend—but could she be a *Disney Girl*?

#2 *Attack of the Beast: Isabelle's Story*

Isabelle's next-door neighbor Kenny has been a total Beast for as long as she can remember. But now he's gone too far: he secretly videotaped the Disney Girls singing and dancing and acting silly at Isabelle's slumber party. Isabelle vows to get the tape back, but how will she ever get past the Beast?

#3 *And Sleepy Makes Seven*

Mrs. Hayashi is expecting a baby soon, and Yukiko is praying that this time it'll be a girl. She's already got six younger brothers and stepbrothers, and this is her last chance for a sister. All of the Disney Girls are hoping that with a little magic, Yukiko's fondest wish will come true.

#4 *A Fish Out of Water*

Ariel in ballet class? That's like putting a fish in the middle of the desert! Even though Ariel's the star of her swim team, she decides that she wants to spend more time with the other Disney Girls. So she joins Jasmine and Yukiko's ballet class.

But has Ariel made a mistake, or will she trade in her flippers for toe shoes forever?

#5 *Cinderella's Castle*

The Disney Girls are so excited about the school's holiday party. Ella decides that the perfect thing for her to make is an elaborate gingerbread castle. But creating such a complicated confection isn't easy, even for someone as super-organized as Ella. And her stepfamily just doesn't seem to understand how important this is to her. Ella could really use a fairy god-mother right now. . . .

#6 *One Pet Too Many*

Paula's always loved animals, any animal. Who else would have a pet raccoon, not to mention three cats, three dogs, four finches, and fish? When Paula finds a lost armadillo, though, her parents say, "No more pets!"—and that's that. But how much trouble could an armadillo be? Plenty, as Paula discovers—especially when she's trying to keep it a secret from her parents.

#7 *Adventure in Walt Disney World:*
A Disney Girls Super Special

The Disney Girls are so excited. The three pairs of *best* best friends are going to spend a week together at Walt Disney World. Find out how the Disney Girls' magical wishes come true as they have the adventure of their lives.